MY TOWN

MY TOWN

WILLIAM WEGMAN

SCHOLASTIC INC.

NEW YORK
TORONTO
LONDON
AUCKLAND
SYDNEY
MEXICO CITY
NEW DELHI
HONG KONG

Chip's homework is to hand in a report on
a subject of his choosing. It's due tomorrow.

TEACHER McMILLAN

The library is a great place to get ideas.

COACH LOMBARDO

The coach always has good ideas. An inspiring pep talk is just what Chip needs.

What about talking to the art teacher? She's creative.

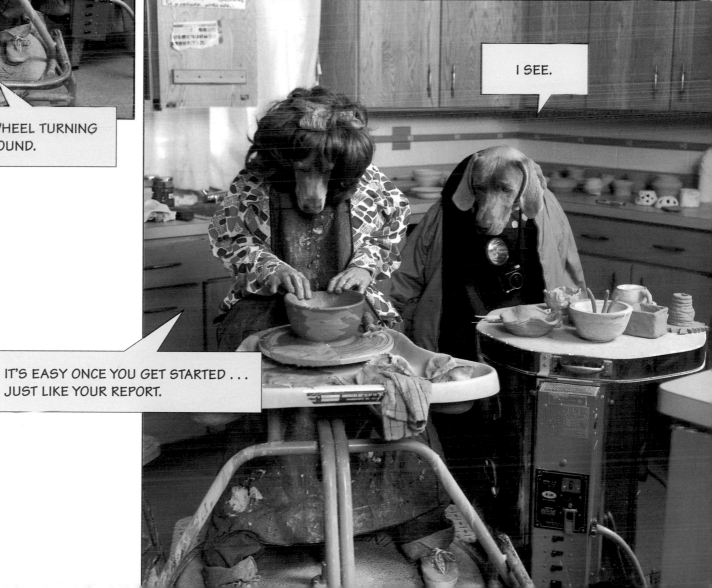

Do *you* have any ideas for Chip?

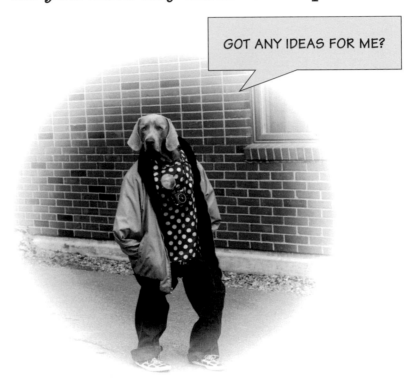

School's out, maybe Chip should go to town.

Ideas come from everywhere. There is no one way. Look in all directions.

Speaking of late, Chip should get zipping
on that report, or he'll never deliver it.

Will Fire Chief Chundo get Chip fired up, kindle his tinder, flame his passion, hose his hesitations?

The situation is really quite alarming. Chip's homework is due **tomorrow!**

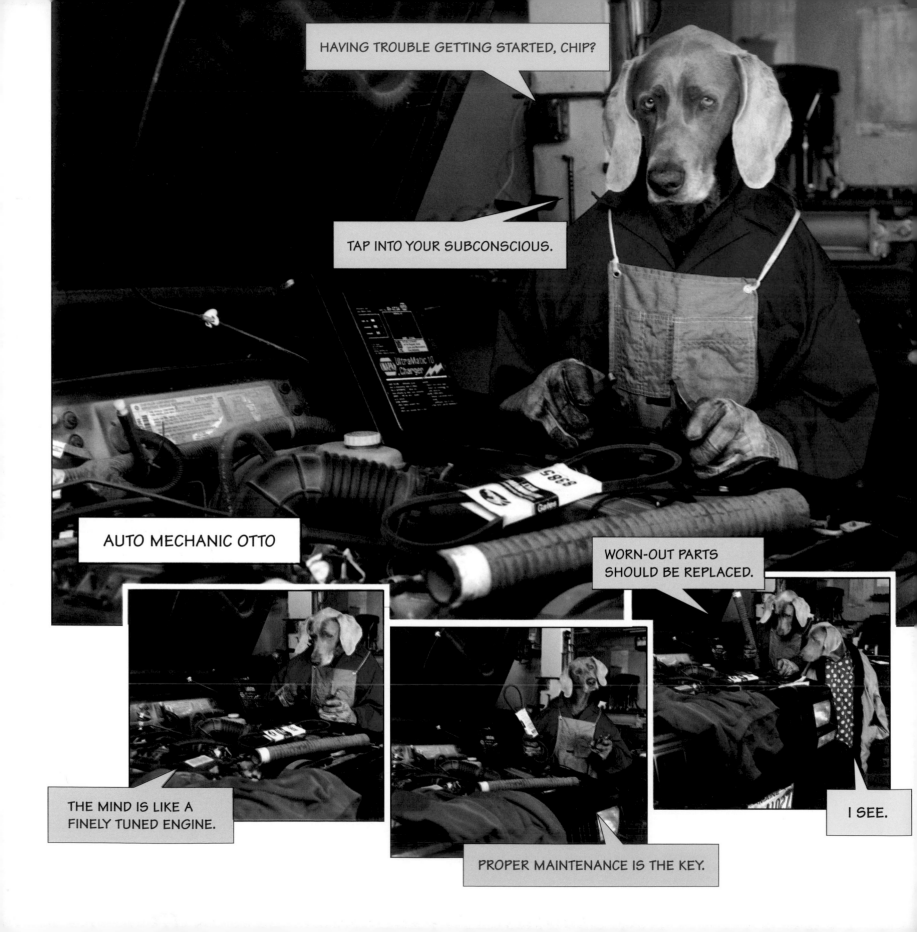

A visit to the auto repair shop and a quick check under the hood may help Chip.

Perhaps getting his hair cut will make Chip think better. Looking good is important.

Chip should check out the supermarket
and shop around for ideas.

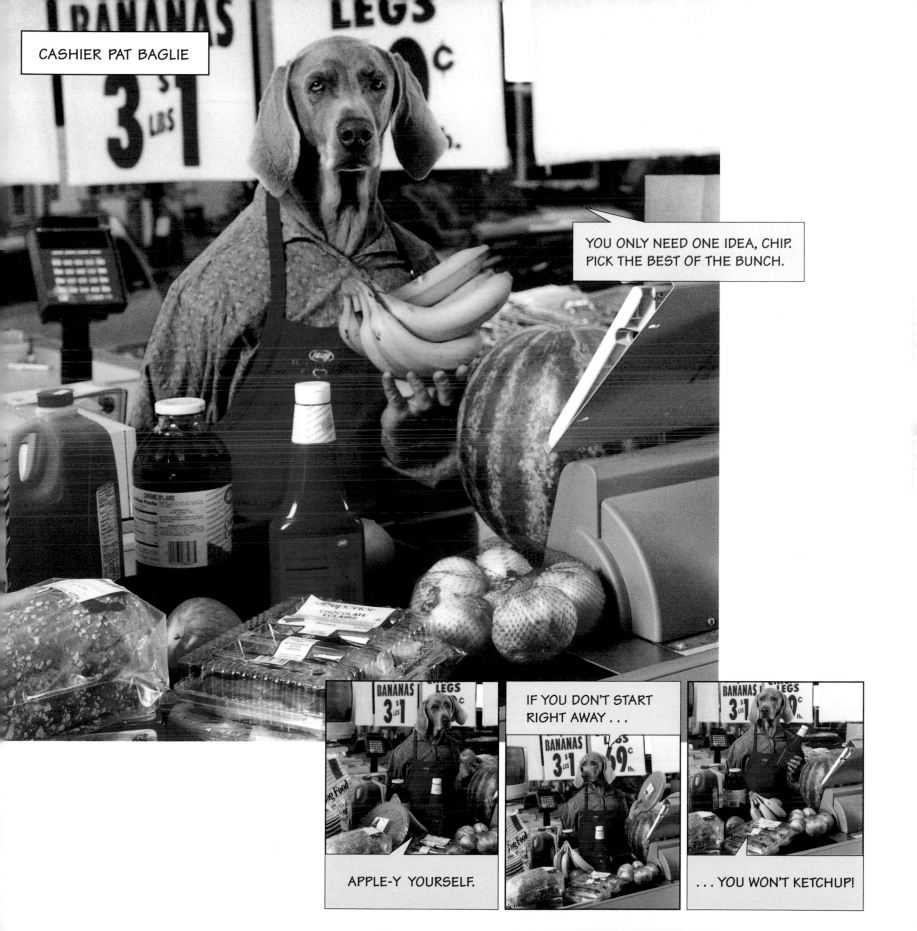

Maybe Chip should see a doctor.

Is Chip okay?

Chip is running out of time. Hey, wait a second . . .

Hey wait a second!

Teacher McMillan didn't say it had to be a *written* report (see page 5).

My Town

portraits
by Chip

A REPORT in pictures
a photo essay

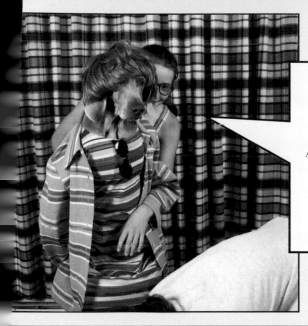

ISBN 0-439-13336-X

Copyright © 1998 by William Wegman
All rights reserved. Published by Scholastic Inc., 555 Broadway, New York, NY 10012, by arrangement with Hyperion Books for Children.
SCHOLASTIC and associated logos are trademarks and/or registered trademarks of Scholastic Inc.

12 11 10 9 8 7 6 5 4 3 2 1   9/9 0 1 2 3 4/0

Printed in the U.S.A.   08
First Scholastic printing, October 1999
Cover photographs © 1998 by William Wegman

DESIGN: DOYLE PARTNERS

THIS BOOK IS SET IN COURIER, CLARENDON, FALSTAFF, GROTESQUE, ROCKWELL, AND TEKTON

ACKNOWLEDGMENTS
WITH MANY THANKS TO THE PEOPLE OF
THE TOWN OF RANGELEY: CHRIS AYLESWORTH;
DAVIDSON'S GARAGE, WAYNE SEEMAN, OWNER;
MEGGAN DAY; MADELEINE DE SINETY; FARMINGTON POST
OFFICE; FRANKLIN SAVINGS BANK AND STAFF;
AMY FREEMAN; DR. JAMES FREEMAN; FRENCHIE;
HOLLY GARNER; SHEPARD GOLUB; SUSAN HAMILTON;
REGGIE HAMMOND; SONJA JOHNSON; BARRY LIBBY, OWNER,
THE BEAUTY BOUTIQUE; M&H CONSTRUCTION; LOONY MOOSE;
JOEY, SHERYL, ASHLEY, BEN, ALEX, AND SHEVER MORTON;
THE MAINE WARDEN SERVICE; ROGER AND PATSY PAGE;
PERFECT PICTURES; POLLUTION CONTROL FACILITY
AT CHICK HILL; RANGELEY FIRE DEPARTMENT,
COMPANY NO. 1; RANGELEY IGA; RANGELEY INN AND STAFF;
RANGELEY LAKES BUILDERS SUPPLY CO.; RANGELEY LAKES
REGIONAL SCHOOL AND RANGELEY LAKES REGIONAL
SCHOOL ART DEPARTMENT; RANGELEY POST OFFICE AND STAFF;
RANGELEY REGION HEALTH CENTER; PRISCILLA AND
BRIAN ST. LOUIS; HAROLD SCHAETZLE, FIRE CHIEF;
CHARLES AND CAROL STEWARD; AND
BOB AND TAMI WENTWORTH.

AND WITH THANKS
FOR ALL THEIR HELP:
STAN AND THEO BARTASH,
ANDREA BEEMAN, CHRISTINE BURGIN,
CRAIG CLARK, STEPHEN DOYLE,
DOYLE PARTNERS, MATT GARTON,
HYPERION, DAVE AND KERRY McMILLAN,
PACEWILDENSTEINMACGILL,
THE PEEBLES FAMILY, HOWARD REEVES,
TERRY ROZO, BRIDGET SHEILDS, AND
KATHLEEN STERCK.

CHIP'S PHOTO ASSISTANTS;
JASON BURCH, SKYE PEEBLES,
JULIE HINDLEY, HEATHER MURRAY,
PAM WEGMAN